For My Mom, God must have known I needed you to love... millions of pennies worth.

Millions of Pennies Worth

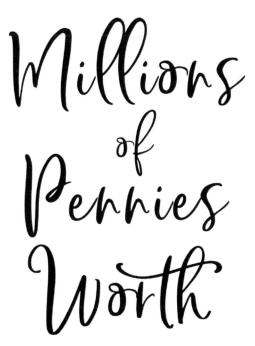

Written By: Amanda Doster

Illustrated by: Emily Larrabee

A new mother lays her newborn daughter Maggie in her crib for the first time. She tucks a blanket tightly around her small body and says, "My darling, I love you millions of pennies worth."

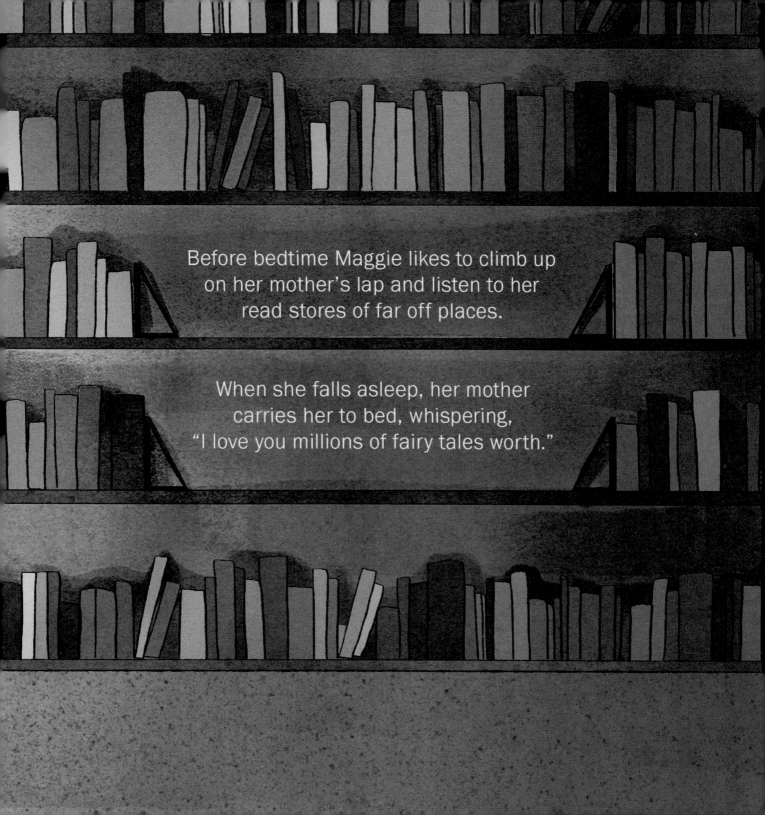

Before bedtime Maggie likes to climb up
on her mother's lap and listen to her
read stores of far off places.

When she falls asleep, her mother
carries her to bed, whispering,
"I love you millions of fairy tales worth."

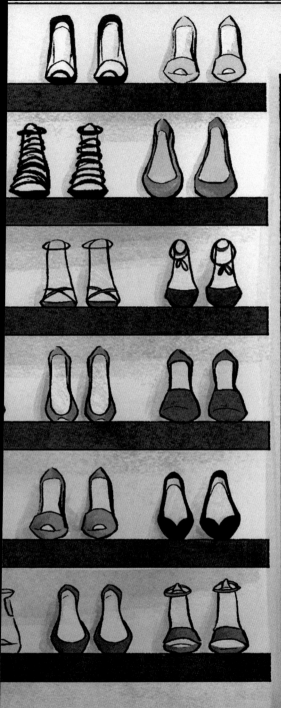

It's not long before Maggie is walking on her own. She loves playing dress up. Her mother helps her into a pair of fancy shoes, saying,
"I love you millions of glass slippers worth."

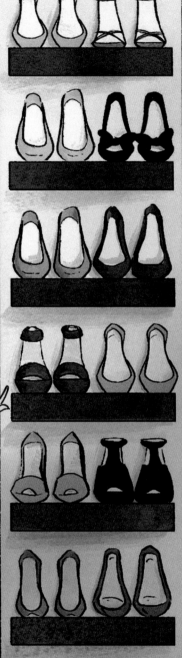

Maggie stood
nervously waiting
for the school bus,
not wanting to let go of her Mom's
hand. As the bus pulls up Maggie lets go.
Her Mom says, with tears in her eyes,
"I'll be right here waiting when you get
home, I love you millions of crayons worth."

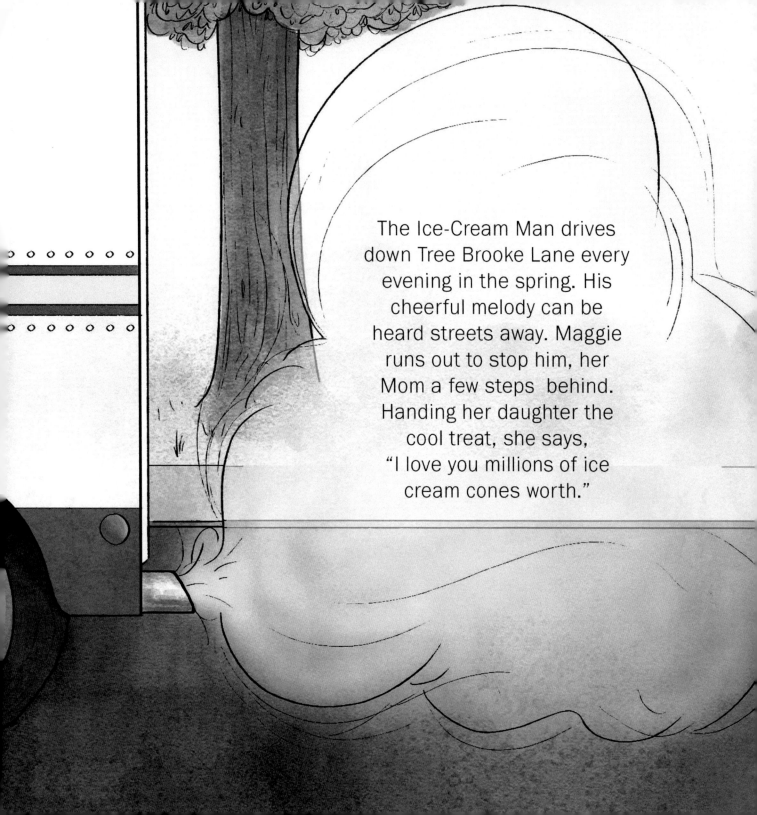

The Ice-Cream Man drives down Tree Brooke Lane every evening in the spring. His cheerful melody can be heard streets away. Maggie runs out to stop him, her Mom a few steps behind. Handing her daughter the cool treat, she says, "I love you millions of ice cream cones worth."

Dressed as Little Red Riding Hood, Maggie sits anxiously on a kitchen stool as her mother applies bright red lipstick to her perfect lips.
As she left to go trick-or-treating, her Mom shouts out the front door,
"I love you millions of lollipops worth."

Soon Maggie is taking figure
skating lessons, and her mother
is watching with such pride as Maggie
leaps, glides and twirls on the ice.
Admiring her daughter's newest
trophy she says
" I love you millions of medals worth."

As a special treat Maggie's mom decides to take her on an outing to get her ears pierced. At the mall they pick out a beautiful pair of dark green earrings. With a gentle squeeze of the hand, she whispers, "I love you millions of emeralds worth."

Summer vacations are spent at the beach.
In the early mornings,
Maggie and her Mom walk
the shore in search of
seashells.

Tossing her a small,
white shell, she smiles.
"I love you millions of
sand dollars worth."

Christmastime comes and Maggie loves to help decorate the tree. As they unpack boxes of decorations, they listen to holiday music. Her mother hands her a sparkling star and says, "I love you millions of Christmas ornaments worth."

For Maggie's Sweet 16 her Mom plans a lovely party for her. There is a beautiful cake covered in buttercream roses. Pink and purple streamers are dangling from the ceiling, and balloons float throughout the room. Presenting her daughter with a small blue box, she says,
"I love you millions of tiaras worth."

Years pass too quickly and now Maggie is going away to college. After settling her daughter in her dorm room, she kisses her forehead and proudly says, "I love you millions of miles worth."

In Maggie's last year of college, she meets a special man. Beaming, she shows her Mom the brilliant diamond on her ring finger. With tears in her eyes, Maggie says, "I love him millions of lifetimes worth."

The Wedding Day comes and Maggie is all smiles getting ready to walk down the aisle.

Looking at her beautiful grown-up daughter, her Mom lightly kisses her cheek and hands her a large bouquet and says,
"I love you millions of tulips worth."

Maggie lays her newborn daughter in her crib for the first time. She tucks a blanket tightly around her small body and says,
"My darling, I love you millions of pennies worth."

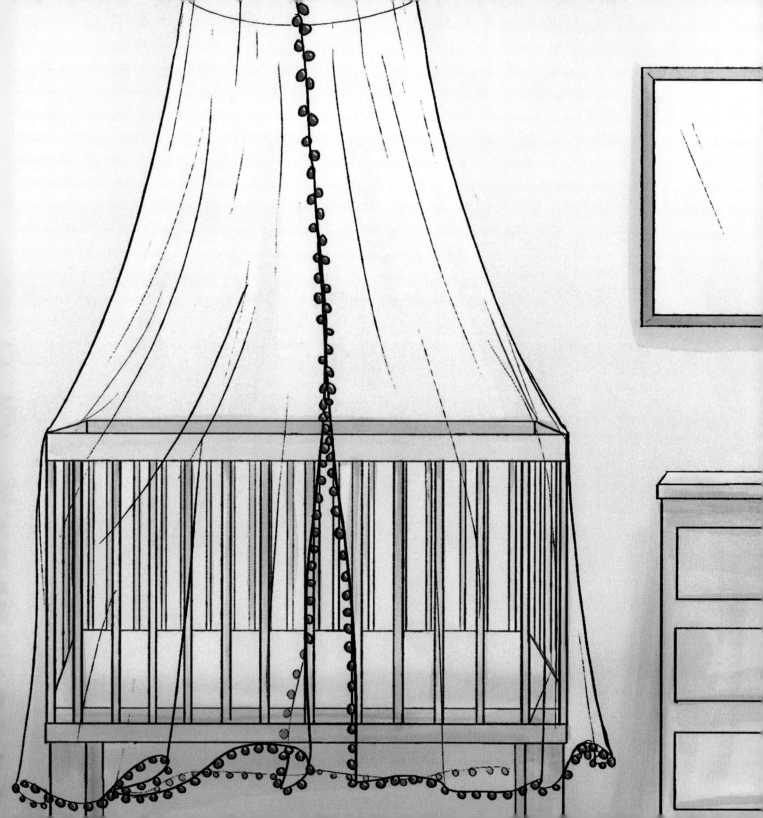

Made in the USA
Middletown, DE
11 August 2019